the sun and her rising

verse is not written, it is bled;
out of the poet's abstracted head.
words drip the poem on the page;
out of his grief, delight and rage."

~ *paul engle*

the sun and her rising

AURA BOOKS

poetry by
kangai benson

mama taught me
not to drag my feet
as i walk through the sands of time
a thirsty soul might come looking
and find their way
to the watering hole

~ *footprints*

to my Maker
my Father
the Almighty God
what can i say?
without You i can do nothing

to my readers
you and i are the poem
i hope i keep writing us

to my family
you make dreaming possible
to my poet daughter Gem
your love for poetry rekindled in me
a fire i thought long dead
here we are

Contents

blue rain 8

hyena dance 58

tangled knots...... 98

liquid fire 124

about the book...... 141

about the author 142

blue rain

thorns used to be my pricking companions
scarring me with black memories
that carried my echo to your nesting silence
you came riding on the morning breeze
and planted blooms
i love the blue blossoms
between my calm fingers
i love the orange blooms
crowning my florid head
i love how they bow phototaxically
towards your speckled light

~ the sun and her rising

she tied the knot with the storm
said *i do* to the boisterous breaking tides
she joined her heart to the gushing river
consummated her love
to the slithering twister
she wedded
knowingly or unknowingly
the steel spade
the wet soil
burying her tired body
alive

~ *she wedded the storm*

sometimes i envy the wind
that gets to caress your face
the sun that gets to kiss your skin
when i can't

~ *missing you*

pregnant blue clouds
beaded with arrogant crystals
whisper heavily into my spongy heart
chilling the ice-cold blood
flowing through my feminine veins

blue rain pouring on my frail form
each drop like a shepherd's whip
the excruciating pain
the only hope of
feeling again

from the other side of hell
she fed him killer mushrooms
then watched his face turn blue
he would rather die in her hands
than in the wild of his jungle

~ *killer mushrooms*

the gawking eyes
the covert looks
unashamedly following our every move

judging miens
hateful glares
that quickly avert when we look their way

their minds wonder
their thoughts speculate

i see through their transparent brains
i hear the whispers of confused souls

answer them
tell them

walk them through
our journey to here
open their eyes
with the sound of your voice
whisper
scream if you must
just tell them
put an end to these endless appraisals

paint the colour of your blood
paint the colour of my blood
on a white canvas
let them tell you the difference
paint me white
paint you black
better still
paint me and you blue

i prefer blue aliens
in a black and white world
than the stares and sneers
than the whispers
concealing their disdain

answer them!
tell them!
will you?

~ *tell them*

the rain is tired of pouring on me
the sun is fed up with drying me

i dug a hole the size of his heart
bowed over and bled him into it
scrapped him from my skin
scooped him from my brain
sewed my heart
wrapped my skin
and walked away in stilts

~ *forgetting*

she used to warm herself on your blazing fire
basking her young heart under your glowing sun
your moon was all she needed in the night
your star shined brightest in her darkness

now your fire has grown cold
your sun is sprinkled with ice
your moon has gone into hiding
your star has fallen into the sea

~ cold fires

coursing through every cell
running down
invading my every sense
like the liquid blood
flowing through my feminine veins
bathing and immersing
my entire being

~ *liquid love*

she could have been his sun
to light his path to far away meadows
he could not stand her piercing brightness
he settled for the moon

the night came
the moon dimmed him further
he groped in the dark
and wished for the sun
only the sun was way beyond
the horizon of his past
quietly mooning over another
in a faraway land

~ he settled for the moon

her petals drip with honey
his bees gather water elsewhere

~ *delinquent bees*

i struggle to see through
the mask of your deafening silence
the cover over your unsmiling face
i struggle to glimpse through
the steel of your heart
the veil over your soul

lines have frozen
on your grim countenance
groom has fallen
on your unmoving lips

i wish i can see
the thoughts on your busy mind
i wish i can know
why the walls have fallen into place

~ *hidden heart*

the sun weeps grey tears
raining on the moon

Lol
as in
love out loud
until the rain started pouring
she could not stand the pressure
he could not handle the measure

his thin filmy skin
could not take the poking
the prodding
the punching
the pricking
of their steel-nailed digits

her dear heart
was straining under the stakes
cracking
breaking
snapping with every insult

until in the end
the viscous blue romance
pooled at their feet
drowning them
in bitter-sweet memories

~ *blue romance*

you and me
the twinning of the moon and the sun

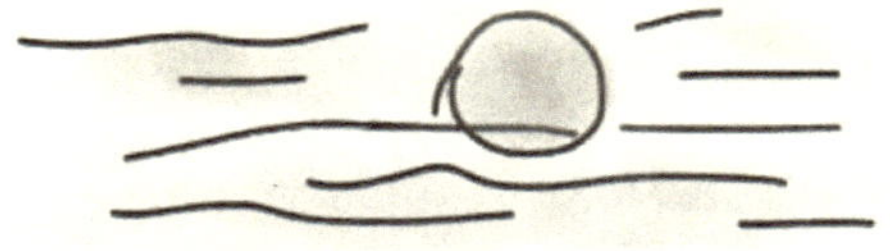

sordid floors
dark paths
lily scented nights
crispy country air
crackling fireplaces

shadows under the moon
sounds of the night
silence of the dark
mingling and tangoing
in perfect pitch
in harmonious beat
of intoxicating drums
and twirling dance
of dizzying village love

~ village love

the ill-tempered brutes come out in line
neigh and bow before her slight majesty
like gentle mules with no stomping strength

she knots their fluffy tails
sets them on orange fire
unleashing their savage spirits
into her burning wild

~ she sure can woo them

i believed he was made only for me
he believed he was God's gift to all

is my mind playing old tricks on me?
or has your colour changed?
i saw you walking down middle street
you looked all white
prim and proper

now at the setting of the sun
at the crawling out of the moon
your full colours seem to bloom
burgeoning before
the nakedness of my watch

you have changed
into a fusion of improper browns and greys
you have even thrown in
some complimentary black

~ *full colours*

his big heart fell from the clouds
shattered into a thousand pieces
terrazzo grains scattered
across the concrete floor
smearing red stains
on her white satin dress
flakes of his flesh
stuck to her virgin feet
he walked away
and got sucked into the storm

~ *heartbreak*

she danced on grey moon
for your dim eyes
sang your tickling songs
to deaf birds

she carried your fiery sun
on her gaunt shoulders
felt your clumsy weight
on her weary back

she held your bleeding hurt
in her soft heart
cried your burning tears
with her tired eyes

she spent wide-eyed nights
for your sleep
waited her life away
for your arrival

today she sits on the ashes
of your burning pride
while you perch your rainbows
on top of the world

~ *waiting for your arrival*

extended blue veins
straining against
my flimsy translucent skin
taut as dry wood
threatening to shred
to break in free eruption
into bloody black riverlets

~ *anxiety*

which revolving door
have you strode through?
where have your hands been?

the shadow of his night lingers
the sun is afraid of it

~ stuck

he emptied her
milked her of herself
one day she floated away
to find herself

the accusations flying
across your taut face
are as clear as september sky
the deep sadness
of your thoughtful eyes
crushing the core
of a heart weak for you

i do not know why yet
but the pain in your eyes
reminds me so vividly
of my sweet mother's breast

i look up to her smiling face
nestling comfortably on her soft bosom
i suckle one soft nipple
the supple tissue tickling my swollen gum

i need to nibble
bite something
the soft flesh of her generous tit
has become my treasured toy

i press harder this time
the pleasure too irresistible
i'm stopped abruptly by a sharp slap

on my small tender thigh
i have pushed the limits i know
things just got out of hand
but i swear by my mother's breast
i never meant to cause you pain

~ *by my mother's breast*

what are you doing here?
his name is boldly emblazoned
on your forehead

he told me i was crass
he told me i was trash
he told me i had no fire
he told me he was tired
he told me
he was leaving me for her

perched on the window of my empty lair
with a half sneer parked on my dry lips
i watched their cute garden wedding
as they strolled on the jacaranda carpet
a picture made in heaven headed to hell

today
she tearfully knocked on my door

he told her she was crass
he told her she was trash
he told her she had no fire
he told her he was tired
he told her
he was leaving her for her

~ they came home to roost

water in all sizes
as dry as midday hell
like crackling summer wood
in the orange bowels
of a screened fireplace
the rich man of lazarus times
has no clue

~ *dry water*

you know they were right
when you see his new garden
watered and full of blooms

~ *moving on*

i love all colours
the golden orange of the setting sun
the red of young roses in bloom
the green of the virgin plains in spring
i love all colours
except the blue hues
painted over my lonely heart

the purple carpet of jacaranda blooms
the white blanket of clouds
over a new april day
the yellow hues of the rising morning sun
i love all colours
except the blue storm
raging over my aching heart

the crystal river rushing down the river
the white of snow-capped tropical mountain
the soft red earth under my tired feet
i love all colours
except the heavy blue shades
of missing you

~ i love all colours

he threw the pot against the wall
she slowly bounced back
she stubbornly lives

~ *unbreakable*

i feel the bitter taste of his breath
on my tongue
i watch the shadow of his former self
stretched like a weary ghost
upon my path

his gaze used to crumble my insides
his voice a healing balm
to my tender heart
his touch sent me flying to the heavens

all he did added beauty
to our paradise
our worlds merged
into one stretch of eternity

i search for something familiar
on the face of the twisted being
glowering at me
i search for the tender eyes
in the deep sockets of this animal
tearing me up
i search for the beautiful heart
that once rested in the void
of his empty chest

i lose focus
the slaps become intense
i slowly open my glassy eyes
hidden under heavy bruised lids

i start to slip
slowly
peacefully
blissfully
i am rising above his voice
i am towering beyond his anger
unfeeling
unhearing
reposeful
serene
numb even

i sense his weak retreat
unsure steps
faltering gait
not pompous stomps of sweet victory
i sense a heavy weight of guilt
on his proud shoulders

i could care less
i will enjoy this lonely spot

i will savour this safe solitude

i watch him unseeingly
his heavy shadow disappearing
in the horizon
of my blissful carefree existence

~ *fallen saint*

wilting flowers
never smelt so great

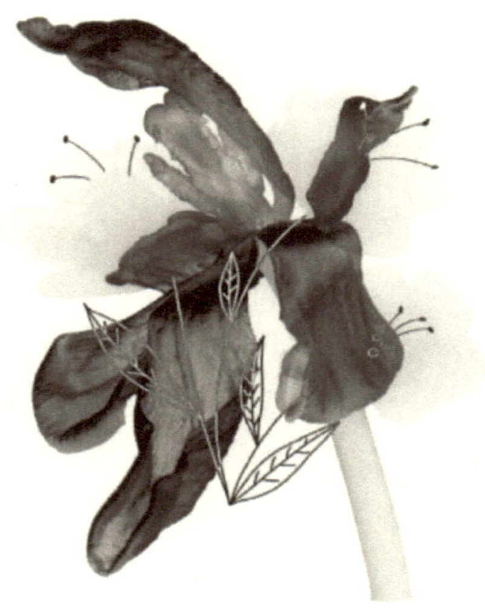

i see your beautiful smile
on the face of a stranger
i hear your soft voice
in the whistling wind of my restless mind
i hear your soothing laughter
in the mingled noises of a boisterous day
i hear your heartbeat
in the heavy thumping of my aching heart

~ *this love!*

his acid sweat burns cavernous holes
through her delicate skin
rancid fumes from the fireplace
waft across her hazed mind
fogging her melting brain

his heart turns sooty under her glaring watch
his icy breath like midnight rain
upon her frozen face
this apparition from a distant land
is slowly becoming
a noxious reality

the wanton feats
the merry laughter
the rash manners
now graduating
with hats too brimmed to be real
all so quietly with no beating drums
into this dull
calm
collected
yawning
organized love

come drift with me to the mountaintops
come dance with me on the treetops
come sing with me in the raindrops
i'll make it worth
your dreamy while

she got him dancing
to the beats of wind
she got him singing
empty melodies from clogged lungs
she got him longing
for meadows and prairies
she got him dreaming
of ocean tides and boisterous seas
she got him talking
of forever and ever

then
she got him taking lonely strolls
in the dark of night
she got him shouting unutterables
in his heavy head
she got him fighting
to get out of his morning bed
she got him shedding blue rivers
in the winter rain

~ she sure got him

bleeding threads
cascading down his wall
a canvas of apparitions
a mural of nightmares
a smiling feminal phantom

~ *memories*

she descends majestically
her crystals glistening
as she lands ever so gently
he hears the sigh of the beaded dust
mingled with the wafting scent
of kilned earth

the parched ground opens its thirsty lips
to welcome the dripping of life
into its bosom
a dry blade of grass rises to attention
aroused by the gentle beating
upon its back

just as quickly as she appeared
she lifts
her glistening beads leave the unsated air
the dry earth still panting with want
longing for just one sip
of intoxicating
summer rain

empty rooms
filled with black nothingness
in the dead of a black humid night
the absurdity of it all
invoking black laughter
from the dry recesses of her heart
like old oil dripping
from an abandoned mine
gushing from her cracked angry lips

~ *emptiness*

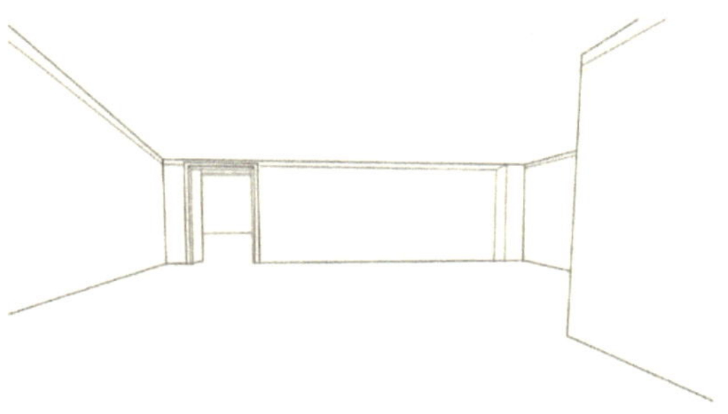

he searched for her among the roses
she looked for him among the mosses
somewhere along the way
they missed themselves

hyena dance

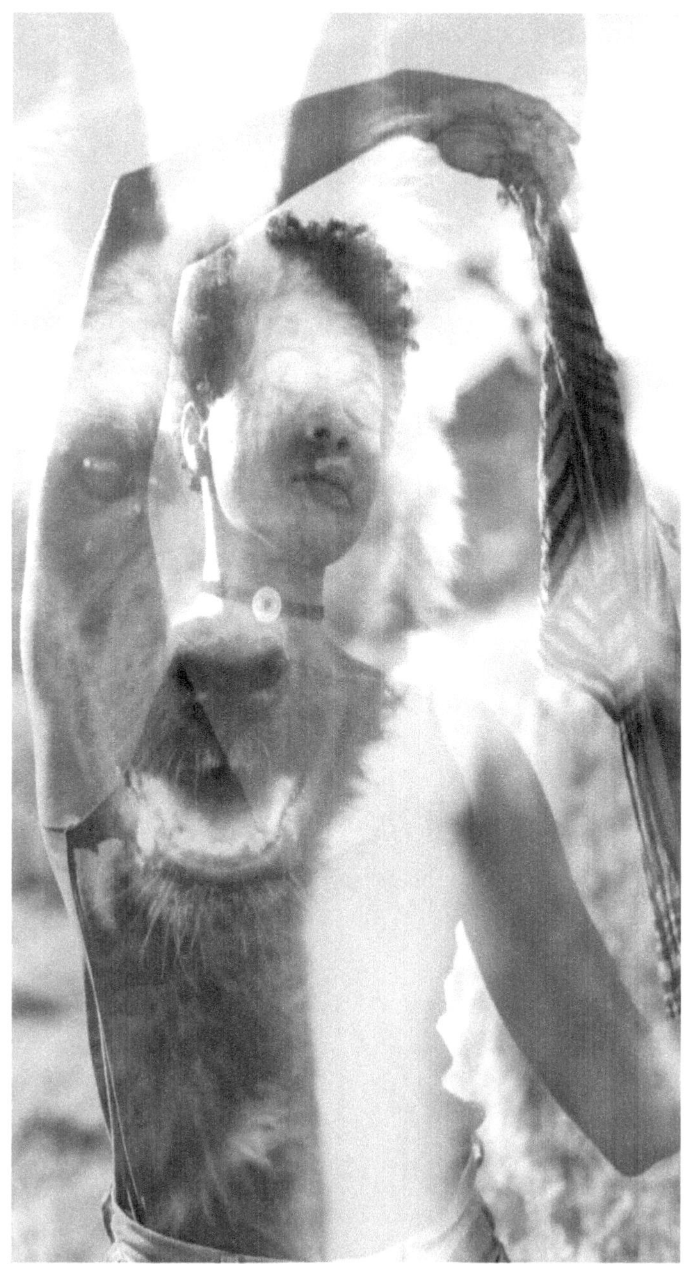

mama did not know
my name betrays me
she would have given me a proper noun
to pompously tag on my proper name

one that would not betray my blood
one that would not deny my kin
one that would secure my plight
one that would be tolerable to rank

~ my name betrays me

protracted gobbling tentacles
straining life out of the gaunt necks
of his hungry subjects

like a dry parched earth
an abyss that is never full
he guzzles down the blood and sweat
of his unwilling prey

a deep gaping pit
an arrogant conduit of all life's finery
flowing unmetered
to his bottomless form
while his trusting subjects
gawk enviously

his victims lie limp
like dead leaves ready to rot
shells of dead wood
long-gone souls
not knowing they created
the monster eating them

~ *corruption*

give some to get some
the ladder is shorter if you do
the journey is longer if you don't
skirts get shorter
brains shrink smaller

~ *it's a dog's world*

they call her the dark continent
though the sun shines brightest on her
black rain pours on her every day
making nonsense of her sun's toil

the twirling tails
the thumping feet
confusing and scaring
the most brave

i am afraid
but fearlessly i dance
to the rhythm of confused intentions
of man and man-eater's midday dance

the lingering scent of my flesh and blood
temptingly wafts over to their hungry senses

i refuse to become their next meal
i dance till the dawn
of the man-made jungle

the dance becomes a slow waltz
their tongues hang out
with exhausted passions

i keenly watch their zombie moves
intoxicated by the wine
of their unstated greed
until they fall over
into a long unwise slumber

~ *hyena dance*

on the coloured blind
of your pitiful mind
your blood looks white
my blood looks black

~ *colour blind*

his formal gait
tailored to impress confidence
his steady gaze
designed to echo thoughtfulness
his handpicked words
organized to sound wise
his slight smile
curated to look important
his perfect suit
styled with hooks to your brain

~ *designer life*

tears of mad gods
thrash down weak shelters
of rotten metal sheets
and polyethene sheds
ghostly scarecrows lined side by side
along dark alleys filled with sewer and filth

these are the first to go under
from the beating down of loony gods
the metal sheets are brutally ripped off
the weak pegs sigh and give way

like feathers the structures are lifted
by the gustily unforgiving wind
exposing their trembling victims
crouched under the open skies

sated and appeased
the wrathful elements dry their tears
the mighty sun comes out in vengeance
scorching and burning
the living and the dead

before long
the dams are empty
fields are dry
flocks are dead

with all we know
we are yet to know
how to tame the crazy gods

~ *loony gods*

"dark continent"
tattooed across her bold behind
in black dripping ink
devoid of white drapes
to the amusement of drunks

"poverty"
etched on her ebony back
in bright golden crayons
bought from the white shop
across her brown mud hut

"corrupt"
branded across her parched hands
a constant reminder
that her sin is more glowing
than the white-washed guilt of west

"backward"
imprinted on her firm breast
her suckling tot would have to see
that years spent in white servitude
rendered her less human

"foolish"
stamped on her pleated brow

with black indelible ink
to match her dark skin and white brain
bereft of a white education

~ *africa*

he struggles and gasps
longing to fill his frail lungs
with just a short gust of now precious air

he writhes and twists
groaning inaudibly in confusion and pain
his chest feels tight
his small form weak with exhaustion

instinctively
unwittingly
he opens his small unused mouth
he swallows and chokes on the thick fluid
that was once his source of life

a battle is raging
in what was once his peaceful home
his world is churning
his being is in turmoil
he is drowning in a fast receding ocean
of a dark unfamiliar world

then suddenly everything stops
he takes one last breath of goodbye
to the world he never got to know
of the cuddle he never got to get

of the laughter he never got to share
of a life he never got to live

~ a life never lived

his gashing wounds bleed from within
his silent moans audible to none
his tears unseen
his cries unheard

the rat-race has taken its toll
the society is his final judge
what he makes proves him a man
who he is does not count
what he drives must be bigger
than his bleeding heart

he has nothing
if he is not spinning the latest
he is a nobody
if he has not perched his
adorable family on the leafy suburbs
he is nonentity
if his adorable brood
is not schooling with princes
he is insignificant
if his beautiful wife
is not driving the sleekest

~ *middle class*

he slithers in unnoticed
noiselessly
a cunning serpent
gliding through the air
a lost ghost of old
invisible
eyes darting
searching in the dark

he takes a few steps
faster this time
at the door he pauses
it's do or die
a few fumbles
a few turns
the lock gives way
the door gives in
he stumbles in
straight to the treasure

a minute later he emerges
under the heavy weight
of valuables and
other less valuables
suddenly
unexpectedly

he crashes down
with a lifeless thump
a timely bullet
shattering his young heart

~ a master of the night

who will cry for him
and all the faceless souls
ripped out of bellies
of innocent
and sometimes
not so innocent girls?

who will search keenly
into their future to see
who they could have become?

then they will no longer be faceless
unworthy of life
we will give them real faces
we will consign them real souls
we will mourn
we will cry
we will stop devouring
the flesh of our flesh

~ *devouring the future*

dropping temples
drooping miens
parched skins
calloused palms
sinewy muscles
hardened lips
wearied souls
roughened feet
a rainbow of emotions
a tapestry of thoughts

~ *toughened ways*

i hear the laughter
drifting from happy children
from the homesteads where mama works
the mwangi's and the okello's
they have it all she says
i wonder what she means by that

mama says
mwangi's daughter rachel is my age
i would like to see her someday
though mama said *no*
i often wonder where she goes to school
what her school is like

mama says
she is very tired today
she talked about scrubbing and cooking
she also talked about the pink bedroom
belonging to rachel
i wonder how it would feel like
to have my own bedroom

mama says
we are blessed to have a roof over our heads
even though when it rains
it is like the roof is not there

wouldn't we be more blessed
with a roof that doesn't leak
or two rooms
with a good roof over our heads?
mama says
okello's children are wasteful
am not sure i understand
there is hardly enough at home
she says we should not complain
after all i get to go to school
there we get to have a meal

mama says
one day our lives will be like theirs
we will have our own home and enough to eat
i believe her
i want to believe her
i pray for her
i pray for my siblings

~ *domestic worker*

a cursed monster that will not be sated
a wide gaping mouth
blood-sucking fangs
ready to eat the flesh
drink the blood and sweat
of emaciated unwilling prey

i toil under the midday sun
month after month
year after year
the monster harvests
leaving some for my empty barn
shortly
the monster comes back
to take his share
of the little he left me

~ *taxes*

is it the emptying of my mind
for western ideals
or the adding to my ideals
what is good from the west?

~ *modern education*

last night my brother did not come home
mama waited the whole night
i wanted to wait with her but i fell asleep
i dreamt she was crying
and praying softly

mama woke up earlier than usual today
i doubt she slept at all
her eyes look red
the way they used to look
every morning daddy came home

daddy no longer comes home
mama says he went to heaven
when he drank something bad
i wonder if daddy fights in heaven
the way he used to fight us
mama says you cannot do bad things in heaven

i can tell mama is worried for my brother
she does not want him to go to heaven yet
she wants him to go back to school
i would also like to see him back in school

mama says my brother does not like school
i do not know if she knows the truth

i heard him tell his friends
he does not mind school
but he needs to work
to help her with rent and food

i wonder if my brother will ever come home
my friend allan told me
what happened to his brother
bad people stabbed him as he walked home
i wonder if allan's brother is in heaven
i wonder if he has met daddy

i do not want my brother
to go to heaven and meet daddy
even though mama says
heaven is a happy place
mama and i need him
more than God and daddy
please God bring my brother home
today

~ *ghetto gloom*

i stand boldly
in rank and wit
before the midday sun
the noise of my tempestuous blood
is louder than johnny's flour mill

you have padded your ears
to the sound of my misery
you have put blinders
against the silhouette
of my unwelcome existence

my screams stain your clear day
my words defile your peaceful night
i haunt your dreams
and gnaw at your conscious

you wish me away
and wake up to find me
seated heavily
on your padded bed

you see
it took me long to get here
it will take you longer to get me going

~ *here to stay*

strutting on neon heels
down cabro-paved streets
my head in the clouds
my nose in the air
my chin on top of the city evergreens
my neck getting longer
with every back-twisting stride
i am on butterfly wings
i am the wispy feather
of a blithe eagle

he has cooked
fed our growing brood
scrubbed the mirror kitchen
he sits with his large heart in his fishing boots
staring unseeingly at the large screen
his waders are shrinking
his heart is sinking

he hopes i am okay
he prays i am okay
he dreads the night
i will not be okay

he is choking
on the hot potato of my freedom

my stilettos are breaking
under the weight of my head
in rancid silence we eat our burnt goose

~ *the goose is overcooked*

he snakes through the heavy morning traffic
like a swift provoked cobra
out on a hunting mission
pursuing a fast and furious prey

he does not care for any rules or laws
no direction is forbidden
he crisscrosses all the four lanes
behind and ahead of speeding motorists

the luggage of willing humans
bundled in multiples the law forbids
swaying left and right
hanging by the grip
of *boda boda madness*

we drink from their calabash full of lies
feast from the stinking pot
of putrid deception
brewed in the minds and meets
of our so-called leaders

the charging buffaloes hook their twisted horns
through our scrawny bellies
dragging our pitiful selves
through maniacal episodes
of euphoric chest thumping
maddening bouts
of pretentious mudslinging
every election year

dazed from knocking our heads
on walls erected for this purpose
we gladly sell our souls
and blindly give our votes
offering them yet another chance
to empty our coffers
into their ever-growing pockets
and ever-enlarging bellies

we then watch in self-pity
as our scrawny children

and malnourished elders
strangle under the grip of hunger
our sick dying of curable maladies
while our kith and kin
spend cold unrelenting nights
in makeshift wooden sheds
and torn metal shacks
unfit for human habitation

~ *putrid deception*

five pairs of hungry eyes
stare dreamingly at my pained face
unseen fingers like sharp nails
pierce unrelentingly
punching holes on my bleeding heart

i plead my innocence
i beg for mercy
they do not seem to care
all they know is the gnawing pain
of their empty bellies
the sound of their rumbling stomachs

i accept the poking
the pain
bind my bleeding hurt
and stare into the black pot
its empty belly defiantly stares back
i place my heavy head in my rugged hands
and cry

~ *empty pot*

step up and speak to my bold face
unwrap you small brain before my fed-up self
drool your words on your narrow chest
let me see the lettery cascade of your bile
the storm behind your pretentious smile

~ *backstabbing*

somebody wake me
shake me
rouse me
from yesterday's dream

yesterday
the rain was generous
the farms were lush
the harvest was heavy
the barns were full

yesterday
there was enough for all and more
the cat and rat ate together
the rich and poor dined like kings
the farmer walked through his farm
a rare twinkle in his quick eyes

today
the earth is scorched dry
dehydrated animals collapse at the roadsides
weary farmers wobble in want
malnourished children play with thin dust
scrawny wives stare into the horizon
dreaming of yesterday

a loving mother carried an angel in her womb
nine months of tears and joy
anticipation mingled with fear

on the momentous day
he was delivered to her uncertain world
she looked at his small form and wept

at six years
the angel came of age
with searing pain she let go
of the one she loved in a way only she could

street urchin
in kenya chokora is his name
the name given
to her precious son

faceless body dripping with black odor
black clothes gleaming in the sun
a beautiful soul hidden way beneath

nobody seems to know
nobody seems to care
that deep within the faceless form
is the little angel she birthed and loved

~ *chokora*

the placid rot of yesterday's blooms
conceal wet mounds of infested soils
amorphous black sheaths
cover unmarked graves
hide bloodsucking tentacles
that leech off inordinate hungry souls
eating flesh and swallowing dreams

~ *politics*

several eyes
stare in unusual alertness
distrust and curiosity play out
on the innocent faces
their small dry mouths fall open
unwittingly betraying the unsaid words
the feelings of wonder
the sense of admiration
the longing for just a flitting contact
with the stranger and her coupé

with one sweep of my eyes
i take it all in
the stench
the garbage
the muck
at the front and back alleys
of rotten iron sheet structures
not fit for human habitation
but home to millions of kenyans
who do not know life any other way

i say a feeble hello
to the now smiling faces
of the faceless children
sons and daughters of our merciless land

like a ghost in daylight
i pause then pass
as i wonder in silent guilt
how such darkness
has not been obliterated
by the sun hanging over our leafy suburbs

~ *dark age*

her shaky hands
scooped and sewed up my womanhood
presented the flakes of my tender gift
on a golden platter
for the elders' approval
i was now a woman

~ *fgm*

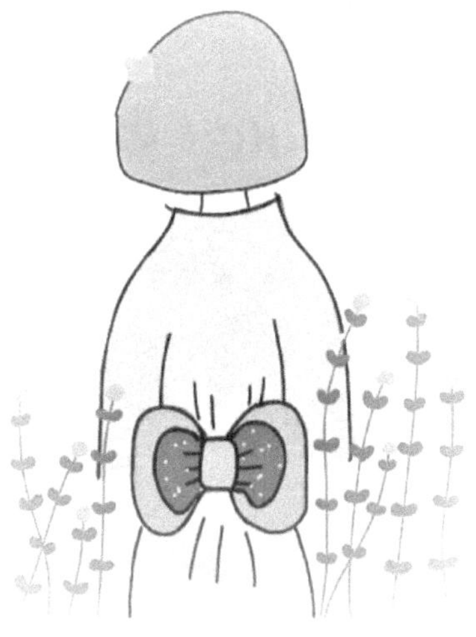

tangled knots

baby coos from the bare pink nursery
drift noiselessly
into the lifeless neighborhood
barnacled tentacles clutch my dry pipes
i swallow the tentacles
they turn bitter in my brooding bowels
pungent sweat drips down my pleated brow

i clutch the shreds of my shattered heart
in the veined palm of my trembling hand
i hurl it fiercely against the staring walls
my grainy heart mates with the ice-cold walls
and breaks into blue rhymes
to sooth the wounded hollow
of my broken heart

~ *blue rhymes*

unrestrained
untempered
he is a child of the wind

she clutches her heart in her wrinkled hands
he carries his head in his tired palms
the child floats above their crouched forms

~ *trouble child*

he nursed on her venom tit
his bile has risen
his tongue fills his mouth

~ *toxic parenting*

humid noxious air
dripping gunk
drilling through her fresh skin
muffling the sound of rough cottons
as her mind wanders

her eyeballs fix on a spot
a moment
a ray in the horizon of her existence
her curled fingers wriggle
and reach out to a time and a place
conceived and pregnant
in the womb of her mind

he rolls away
sighing with throaty noises
with only his rusty scent
to bring her back from neverland

~ *kin (un)love*

the nursery man said they were tomato seeds
with a self-assured grin
he watered them with the sweat of his brow
fertilised the soil with the juice of his toil

everyone knows tomatoes are red
right?

only they turned out to be bastard tomatoes
no way he could have slaved to breed
these black-streaked monsters

~ *bastard tomatoes*

where she used to grow green
to feed her adorable angels
black blossoms now bloom
their black twines covering the ground
black petals swaying softly
in the grey breeze of day

she tends the blossoms religiously
their musky scent
massaging her weary senses
crusty teardrops glistening
on her wrinkled face
black memories
flooding her aging mind

it seems like yesterday
they were a young bubbly lot
she could have sworn
before the Almighty
she had done right with them

then the black wind
that unrelenting storm
swept mercilessly
across her dusty homestead
burying them all

next to each other
the black blossoms
stoically taking their place

~ *black blossoms*

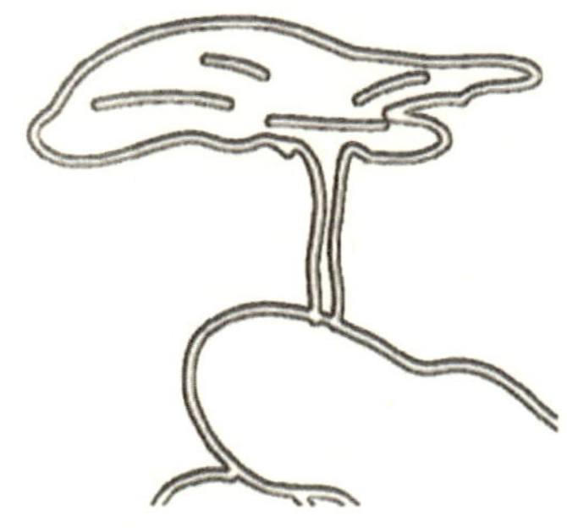

twisted untangleable knots
of all colours
running through our skins
our brains
our blood
tying us intricately and haphazardly
a complex mass of tight ropes
cording me
you
in an endless dance of life
and i wonder
death?

~ *kin*

her crusty blue brush paints all colours black
her looming grey clouds cover the sun

she kills slowly
softly but sure
like dripping mercury
like drooling acid
flowing lazily from a broken pot
drilling icy holes
eating up flesh
drowning life
bleeding air
out of the lungs of the living

~ *cantankerous woman*

they flow down long ebony necks
in all colours
textures and lengths
curly
straight
long
short
black
blond
brown
red
some natural
others quite unreal and eccentric
against the gleaming ebony skins
of stunning african queens

~ *hair weaves*

she walks blindly and stumbles
rises and falls
lost in the stormy night
black clouds covering the brooding moon

she reaches out and catches her foot
falls into the muck and dirt below

a scream escapes from the deep recesses
of her frail being
the sound unexpected and alien
in the dark of night
like a drop of ice in the eerie of hell

she knows nobody can hear her
irrespective
she continues screaming
the sound of her deep groans
proving she is alive if nothing else
the release surprisingly welcome

~ *leaving*

guttural rending
wrenching animal groans
the inexplainable crashing pain
of her shredding insides
churning
violently breaking
as the smallest of humans
seeks to break free
from the safe prison
of her motherly protection

~ *motherhood*

she runs on lames
she crawls if she must
she can be down but not out
she can be sleeping but awake and aware

she sees in tangible darkness
hears amidst deafening noise
nothing misses her watchful eye

she will cry for joy and laugh in sorrow
she will embrace in hurt and let go in love

with a soft heart she cuddles
with a firm hand she disciplines
with a hearty laugh she loves
with a nippy eye she admonishes

they unwittingly call her the weaker sex
for her strength cannot be quantified
it is not measured by muscle or bone
but the gentleness of her cuddle
the firmness of her hands and heart
the swiftness to rescue and heal
the bubbly laughter of her caring soul

~ *enigma*

he creeps in unnoticed
veiled in saintly regalia
into the lives of those we love
at first their friendship is easy and cordial
sip after sip the friendship scales start to tip
from mutual to dependency
from easy to demanding

thoughts of their next encounter preoccupy him
his limbs get weak
his head gets heavy
he sets out in a dazed state of regret
to look for his daily companion

his coffers are empty
well-wishers come in handy
or payback of a favor owed
he gulps down the dark brown liquid
or the clear illegal fluid
depending on the day's fortunes

he wakes up drenched
somewhere in a trench
stinking muck flowing over his weak self
he throws up into the passing effluent
the stench hanging onto him
his insides churning within

i need help
he mutters to himself for the millionth time
but first to wambui's den
tomorrow is as good a day to seek it
little does he know
for him and his buddies
tomorrow will never be

~ *vicious friend*

do not be fooled
by her white smile
contrasted by ebony skin
do not judge this book
by the cover of her pages

do not be duped
by her full-figured swagger
her hearty laughter
seemingly of no care

her heart is strong
her love is vibrant
her rage as boisterous
as her stormy mirth

she will fight if she must
she will run because she must
she will stay
because she wants
to love you in the storm

her heart
like an angel
her wrath
a gathering storm

her smile
a soothing balm
her grip
as strong as a vise
her touch
a baby's sigh
her limbs
swift as a deer
her love
a gentle breeze

~ *the ebony force*

broken dolls
salvaged from the trenches
and garbage mounds
of yesteryears

too blind to see
too deaf to hear
too dumb to talk
too numb to feel

floating ghosts
under hot september sun
flapping weak wings
in the direction
of the winds

until
He picked them up
lifted them up
raised them up
pumped them up
with life from His very soul

today
the once lifeless dolls
are full of life

they walk and talk of Him
and Him alone

~ salvaged

the toothless giggle
one tiny smile of a little child
shedding rays of sunshine
awash my easy heart

the kindness of a passing stranger
the shoulder of a friend to lean on

the little things
that lets me know He knows
that lets me know He cares
that He works in mysterious ways

~ the little things

do not struggle to untangle me
i was not meant to be understood
i am eternity stretched beyond time
what is mortal cannot unravel the eternal

i am not the colour of my skin
i am not the shape of my nose
i am not the sound of my name
i am not the size of my brain
i cannot fit in the mold of your taxonomy

the ocean belly hides much
below her fleeting surface
only her Maker knows
the depth of her bosom

you cannot measure my eternal essence
with a span of your rational eyes
or the lingering attempts to unstitch me

i am beyond the limits of your mind
i am beyond the sphere of your kind
what is mortal cannot unravel the eternal

~ stretch of eternity

broken and discarded
You poured Yourself into me
Your love sealed all the cracks

~ *restoration*

bitter heart
bitter thoughts
bitter words
dripping
pouring like october rain
pooling languidly
sending back putridness
like an old toxic well
killing the master
and the subject alike

~ *toxic old wells*

i dance to the beat of her song
twirl to the whoosh of her skirts
i elatedly belt out her carefree tune
smile at the touch of her breeze
i sigh at her whisper of my name

she lifts and tosses me in the air
i land shamefacedly on the ground
never to trust the wind again

~ the luring wind

liquid fire

LET your
DREAMS
Set Sail

mama taught me
not to drag my feet
as i walk through the sands of time
a thirsty soul might come looking
and find their way
to the watering hole

~ *footprints*

in the closet of her hungry mind
she weaved lofty dreams
rainbow threads
towering and mounting
pregnant mosaics of her restless mind
resplendent tapestries of her fertile wit
she stepped back and loved the colours

then she slept
a tooth-full smile stuck between her full lips

she dreamt
a dream that would take her to wits end
a spotted incorrigible hyena
with snorting laughter on his lips
was peeing rabidly on her rainbow dreams

~ he peed on her dreams

i caught my foot on treetops
spinning reeds with weaver birds
when i could have been
flapping wings with eagle birds

passions of yesterday
passions of today
passions of tomorrow
tugging at my untamed heart
pulling at my unclipped wings
beckoning me to sail into the clouds

my wings flutter
my heart skips a beat
my eyes wander longingly
at the motioning light clouds
my belly is burning
with unquenched liquid fire

i now know there is no reprieve
i now know there is no rest
until i quench this raging fire

~ *liquid fire*

she walked with roosters
long enough to see
chicken speckles on her eagle face

deep down the village alley
camouflaged by dark shadows
of impervious moonless nights
young girls lose their virginity
as easily and as fast
as baffled farmers
lose their arrow roots
to the village wag

deep down the dark belly
of the village alley
young men snort away dull evenings
and bright futures
losing their innocence to illicit pleasures
and illegal substances

deep down the village alley
yesterday's dreams
have become
impossible mirages
for today's youth
the village alley has now become
the infamous alley of lost dreams

~ *the village alley*

silent moans
inaudible groans
held back in empty tombs
of regrets
of what-ifs
of what could have been
but is not

~ tombs of what-ifs

i look down
at the obscure pool of dreams
lying below my straddled legs
like tattered un-shapely garments
plastered with aged sweat streaks
dripping with dry tears
broken threads running bare
across the old rugs
that were once beautiful tapestries
carried across many oceans
to the land of empty dreams

~ *broken dreams*

i am a butterfly
i am changing
and it is okay

~ *growing*

she livened the world with her songs
one day the hippo heard her sing
he looked up and insulted her beak
she stared at her reflection in the water
the hippo was right
she was one ugly fowl
she was one ungifted bird

she swore never to come out again
she swore never to sing again

while she sits still
the world is silent
waiting for nightingale to sing

each time she fell she grew

wide eyed
tails wagging
ears straining
slyly they tiptoe around me
soundlessly circling my privacy
picking potent seeds
scattered within my busy wits
i wake up to lush fields
planted and growing
seeded with my secret dreams

~ *the apes*

we see his dawn
not his dusk

we see his glory
not his story

we see his rainbows
not his rain

we see his success
not his failures

we see his victories
not his battles

before the glory
there is a story

before the morning
there is a night

~ story to glory

does my candle dim your light?

grass grows under her heavy feet
she refuses to move
until he comes to mow
and move her

~ *mind sets*

the sun and her rising
is a collection of poems about love
that is often like a rose flower:
magnificent in its beauty
but burdened with pricking thorns
it is also about the intricacies
of family relationships and the
socio-cultural, spiritual, economic,
and political complexities
of life in the contemporary world

the book is split into four chapters:
blue rain, hyena dance,
tangled knots, and liquid fire

about the book

dr. kangai benson is a poet,
inspirational blogger and entrepreneur
her leisure time is spent
experimenting with cooking recipes,
traveling, reading,
listening to music, and dancing
she lives in nairobi, kenya
with her husband and four children

about the author

9 789914 701838